MW01257814

Everything Was Fine Until Whatever

A Book of Stuff
by Chelsea Martin

Future Tense Books
portland, oregon

(This book had a number of titles attached to it during its production. They were: *Your Secrets Are Funny, Some Mean Wishes, Off To Therapy, Really Though, You're Welcome, Nice Syntax Kind Of, The Kiss-Ass Olympics, Here's Some Awkward Tension and Transparent Compliments, Untitled Cos I'm Blackout Drunk A Little, Impulsive Kite Flying, Paranormal Shower Drain Findings, Startling Photos of Death-Comets Coming Toward Us, The Outsiders, Orange You, Seems Like No One Singing, I Practically Never Want to Harm You, Pains In The Asses, Real Flattery, Too Too Much*)

Everything Was Fine Until Whatever
by Chelsea Martin
Copyright 2009 Chelsea Martin
and Future Tense Books
ISBN-10: 1-892061-35-X
ISBN-13: 978-1-892061-35-5
First Printing: April 2009

Some pieces previously appeared (usually in a slightly different form) in: *See You Next Tuesday, Young Revolutionaries,* and *Zygote in my Coffee.*

Cover and interior artwork by the author
Book design by Jenn Lawrence
Type set in Cochin

Future Tense Books
PO Box 42416
Portland, OR 97242
futuretense@q7.com
www.futuretensebooks.com

I WANT TIME TO GO BY VERY SLOWLY AND FOR ME TO DIE QUIETLY IN MY SLEEP IN THE BACK ROOM AT WORK WITH LIQUOR BOTTLES ALL AROUND ME, AND CONCRETE EVIDENCE THAT I WAS TRYING TO STEAL THE FAX MACHINE.

Dear Readers,

I want you to think I'm a part of you somehow, or that we share something no one else could possibly understand. I want this to make you a little nervous. I want you to think I'm doing something no one else can do. I want you to think that no one else could do what I do correctly. I want you to spend your money on me. Not all your money, and not necessarily a large amount, but some sort of spending so I know I'm worth something. Hopefully at least three dollars cos if you think about it, what can you get for less than three dollars? I want you to think about me when I'm not around. I want you to think of me, in a non-sexual way, when you're in bed at night. I want you to cry and then realize the absurdity in this emotional release. I want you to laugh through tears and then realize the heartbreaking honesty audible in your laughter. I want your heart to break from seeing so much of yourself in me, and to break again when you realize I know more about you than you do. I want your heart to be so broken that all you can do is pathetically alter yourself in response to my more accurate vision of you and, with unobstructed spirit and determination, love me. I want this love for me to be your only talent, and I want you to eventually realize that it isn't even adequate, and that I really deserve better.

Love,

Chelsea

CON

1   Baby's First Words

10   I understand that 'love' is a word with a definition that interpret differently than others do

11   And I understand that the definition of the word 'love' is filled with words that also have definitions

13   20 Simple Makeup Tips for the Everyday Woman

15   His Lies Taste like Eggs Benedict

16   God's Girlfriend

18   Beginnings That Lead to Middles

21   Maybe Her Pending Corpse is a Window

27   I know what you're thinking. You're thinking I shouldn't work in customer service.

28   I try to drink coffee and look out of windows but eventually I have to crap or blink.

30   Nothing Can Make Me Feel Sincere Not Even True Love.

31   It Could've Been a Photograph of Anybody.

32   I'm Not Drunk, I'm Big-Boned.

33   I write poetry because if I don't I will have to think about serious things.

34   Maybe I'm laughing while I write this because I have no capacity to take anything seriously.

35   Even on Christmas I try to be in a text message conversation at all times.

36   I have started a band and my gimmick is I only write songs about the neighbor's dog and pretend to be displacing my emotions.

37   Is Everyone Ready to See My Muscles?

38   The moral of the story is, do you think I'm fat?

39   I want to text message my mom something cute like *I met a boy*, which is why I'm wearing makeup today.

43   What Are You Wearing!

44   Fable

45   Deer Grazing

46   Your Only Memory of Him

TENTS

Held Together Wrists 49

I'm writing about love because no one else ever has and because I'm wearing jeans that make my butt look good 51

Aftermath of the 90's 54

Telescope 55

WTF QT Sup 56

The Protagonist 58

Manipulation, Energy Drinks, and Time Travel 62

Problems 64

Girls' Guide to Boyfriends in Bathrooms 65

I $ You 67

Kurt and Courtney 70

Aphorism 71

Life is Time Consuming 72

Acronyms To Expedite Conversation 74

Pfeiffer 76

To Do List 80

Do you want me to be sincere or do you want be to be myself? 82

Hats for Dummies 84

Narnia 88

My Biggest Claim to Fame 89

Cousins 90

Wait, Why are You in Denial? 97

Insecurities in Cuties 98

If You Were Wondering if You're a Selfish Asshole 99

Puberty 102

How to Save Money on Your Car Insurance 104

More Perfect and Less Idealistic 106

Today is the Worst Day of My Entire Life (I Always Live in the Present) 108

What the Tabloids are Saying About Me 111

Everything Was Fine

Baby's First Words

June 16– My parents gave me a 'Baby's First Words' journal. When I unwrapped it from its packaging, Baby took one look and said, "Obviously imported from China."

June 17 – Baby called me by my first name today. "Ned," she said, "It's story time."

June 18 – I forgot to take a towel in to the bathroom with me when I showered, and had to run across the front room naked to fetch one. Baby: "What the?" I dutifully sat down and gave her the sex-talk. Glad that's out of the way. I didn't mention to her that her future spouse may ignore her sexual advances for months on end. I thought we could talk about that later, when maybe I would have some advice to give her. Or I could make Karen talk to her about that and listen in on the conversation for insight.

June 19 – Today Karen and I discussed what I would do about my being laid off. I explained we might have to live with less for a while, until the jeans market became popular again. Baby said, "Jeans are so 1970." Karen expected me to be able to adapt my sales talent to other products. I told her she should check back into the real world. Baby chimed in by saying, "Yeah, lady, I heard you cried to *Titanic*."

June 20 – She didn't say anything today, but when I put Baby in her crib for a nap, she crossed her arms and wouldn't take a bottle. So I picked her back up, dressed her, and took her to the park to impress the women there, which is her favorite thing to do. But I was thinking perhaps Karen and I need to start curbing these early signs of manipulation.

June 21 – I took Baby to the city park today. Baby

seemed to get a kick out of yelling out, "Hey, Legs" to the attractive women.

June 22 – My friend and ex-coworker Steve came over today to deliver my last paycheck and I invited him to eat dinner with us. I explained that I was actually happy to be out of the jeans business before jeans became embarrassingly unpopular. Steve said, "You shouldn't judge the cat's pajamas if you can't sell them." What the hell does that mean? Steve is an asshole.

June 24 – I bought Baby plastic 'Mom and Dad' dolls that resemble Karen and I. When I gave them to her, Baby immediately started hitting the two dolls together passionately, saying, "Love is real." Karen doesn't like the dolls. She said I shouldn't have bought them. I think she hates seeing representations of our bodies connecting so dynamically.

June 25 – Baby didn't talk today, but, when prompted, she gestured to me that she preferred the taste and texture of Swiss when compared to bleu cheese.

June 26 – We went to Steve's house today to swim. Karen was venting very flirtatiously to Steve about the 'overwhelming heartbreak' she was supposedly feeling. Steve said, "If you love the ball that's in your court, set it free." Karen said, "I feel unstable. I wish Ned was more attentive to our needs." Noticing the irony of Karen's statement, and acknowledging that I'm the only one who is ever sexually attentive in any way, Baby laughed and said, "Ain't that some shit."

June 27– Today, Baby and I went to the park, but sadly there were no women there for us to impress. I suggested we go home and try to impress Karen. Baby said, in a tone that reminded me of cable television, "Riiiiiiight."

June 28 – Today Karen brought up the fact that I didn't believe she was pregnant with Baby until her second trimester. I reminded her that she was not innocent of faking things. This riled her up and she cried, a throwback to our teenage years together. I felt the same undeserving longing for her that I felt when I first met her. Baby woke up from her nap and said, "Something feels different. Did you guys pump the breast milk without me?" I thought it was an interesting thing for her to say because we have never pumped the breast milk. Karen was upset that I questioned Baby. She has the idea that Baby doesn't need to hear that she's ever wrong, and that we should humor her even when she's spreading totally completely inaccurate information.

June 29 – I gave Baby coffee this morning because she said, "I'm sick of breastfeeding." But she didn't seem to like the coffee either. She sucked it up her straw only to blow it back through onto the cat and Karen's purse, which I noticed is new. When did she get a new purse?

June 30 – Baby tried to grab the chocolate cake I was eating for breakfast, and when I told her she couldn't have any, she said, "Oopsies," and then took off her diaper and pooped on the kitchen floor. I left it for Karen, so she would see what I mean about Baby's seriously inventive manipulation tendencies.

July 1– Baby wanted her diaper changed today. As I changed it, she looked up at me and said, "Story of my life." At first I thought she was referring to the unpleasant consistency of crapping day in and day out, but she explained that even though each crap seems like a huge loss of material and sustenance, the important elements of a meal remain within, that there are remnants of material that never leave us, like a sourdough that keeps being added to, and contribute to the growth and well-being of our bodies, which in effect help form the 'stories of our lives.'

July 2 – Baby wanted her diaper changed again today, but instead of crying and pointing to her diaper melodramatically like she usually does, she sighed and said, "No pain, no gain," and didn't bring it up again until I finished taking my nap.

July 3 – Steve came over today. I can tell Baby doesn't like him. She'll laugh and play when Steve is around, but as soon as he leaves the room, Baby goes, "Tight wad, breath like asshole, let's eat out." At one point, Steve came to me and said, "Ned, what's your secret? You act ten years younger than anyone your age," which really set Baby off. "Loosen up," she said, and rolled off the cushion she was propped up against. I gave Steve some coffee with laxatives in it, but I don't know what happened. I haven't heard anything about it.

July 4 – After updating my internet profile, I stepped into the kitchen to hear Baby say, "Onion." This excited Karen for some reason. She laughed and screamed and encouraged Baby to say it again. "Her first word, her first word," Karen yelled at me, "She said 'Mama!'" I told her that Baby had actually said "onion." This upset Karen, who obviously needed confirmation of Baby's affection towards her. But Baby stuck up for me by laughing and saying, "Onions are really weird."

July 7 – Tonight it was my turn to make dinner. Right after I got off the phone with Dominos, Karen shooed me out of the room. From the toilet, I overheard her using her sexy voice and came out prepared to scold her for talking sexy to Baby. But Baby was sound asleep on the sofa. That's when I realized Karen wasn't talking to Baby; she was on the phone with someone. I pretended I didn't hear her, and asked why she didn't let me touch her hands or lower back in public anymore. I remember saying 'Let's learn to love again,' and her saying something insulting about 'what we've become.' Baby woke up and said, "Dinner is a four-letter word."

July 9 – Karen wanted 'time to think,' which probably means 'time to practice infidelity' this weekend, so I am staying in a motel. I talked to Baby on the phone tonight and she said, "Stuck washing dishes thanks to you."

July 10 – I talked to Baby on the phone again today. I told her about how I'm was thinking about her all day because I saw a lot of women that I just knew Baby could really impress. Baby said, "Shh, TV's on," which was really cute and made me homesick.

July 11 – I came home today and Baby was lying on the living room floor looking really bored. I tried to pick her up, but she pretended to be asleep. When I walked away, she opened her eyes again. She seemed irritated. "Are you mad at me?" I asked. She said, "No, I've just grown quiet because I'm trying to crap."

July 13 – I feel depressed. I haven't talked to Baby or Karen today and I don't think I will. Karen has not attempted to talk to me all day. She looks at me when she's passing through rooms, which makes me think she's not mad. It is as if nothing is wrong and she just doesn't care to talk to me. It is about 10pm and I am watching a show about sharks. The weather is good.

July 17 – Today while I was at home spending time with Baby, I tried to write an apology letter for Karen, explaining that I didn't feel I had anything to be sorry for but I was tired of fighting with her, but Baby ripped it out of my hands and pulled it into the bath-tub. I started writing another letter explaining how I felt and the main reason I was upset, which was I felt like she had turned into some kind of weirdly responsible, conservative adult, which was never our plan.

July 18 – Today I called Baby and I heard Karen talking to someone in the background. "Who is there with you guys?" I asked. Baby told me it was a man who was "funny yet good-looking." I asked her if she happened to catch his name and she said, "Are you sobbing into the receiver?"

July 23 – Karen let me come home again two days ago. Steve was over when I arrived at home after job-hunting today. He tried to shake my hand as I came in, but I explained that this was probably the worst time of year to be exposing myself to rashes or skin diseases. Then we all watched *Nick at Nite*.

July 25 – The small things in life are what impact you the most. I have noticed that when little things of mine are moved from one place to another in the house, I become upset. It has significance because I know Karen is moving these things and I can't understand why. My belt that I had taken off in the kitchen had been moved from one bar stool to another. It doesn't make a difference where it is but it's just that it was a decision made by Karen. Somehow the placement of my belt mattered to her in some way and she needed more control over it.

July 30 – Today Baby said, "Life's flashin' before me and shit." Upon inspection, I saw that she had her first tooth coming in.

August 3 – Today Baby and I took a walk in the park. "Daaang," she said, as a woman with a dog walked by. This pleased the woman, and she came over to us and introduced herself as Aida. "You like the puppy dog?" the woman asked Baby patronizingly. "She said 'dang,'" I explained, "And I think she was referring to your fascinating bosom." "Yeah, Dog," Baby said sweetly, to protect Aida from embarrassment.

August 5 – Today Karen and I both stayed home all day to spend time with Baby. Baby crawled a little around the living room and sat herself in the corner to poop. "Baby," I said, attempting to impress Karen, "what's four plus nine?" "Thirteen," Baby said. "What's four minus nine?" "Negative five," Baby said. "Very good. What's four times nine?" "I don't know yet," Baby said. "She doesn't know her times tables yet," I whispered to Karen. "Ned," Karen said, and looked at me with her disturbed little frown, the way she had been looking at me the whole time Baby and I were solving math, "You're the one who doesn't know your times tables." She's always trying to make things seem like my fault. I never see her teaching Baby math functions, but she would never blame herself, would she?

August 8 – Baby and I went over to Steve's house today. We looked through his windows. We saw a blinking light on the answering machine and a sweater that looked like Karen's. Baby said, "Does this mean I am an orphan?" I said, "No, no, no, you just have a broken family." We climbed a tree so that we might see down into windows without anyone seeing us, but the trees Steve has in and around his yard are particularly lush and it is impossible to see through the foliage.

August 10 – I woke up to Baby screaming hysterically from her room. I went to see her and she had crawled out of the crib and couldn't figure out how to get back in. I picked her up and put her back in the crib and caressed her little head. "Am I the only one that loves you?" Baby said. "No, of course you aren't," I said. "Am I the only one in your life who it is possible to comfort?" she said. "No," I said. "Absolutely not." She shook her rattle absentmindedly and I could see that her knowledge of me was thorough, that she could tell I was lying, and that she didn't feel sorry for me. "Well, " I said. "Looks like Baby needs her first haircut."

SOMETIMES I FORGET WHY I'M SO NEGATIVE AND JUDGMENTAL AND THEN I REMEMBER.

I understand that 'love' is a word with a definition that interpret differently than others do

I dated a boy who wouldn't have sex with me for a long time because he said he liked me too much and didn't want to ruin anything.

When we finally had sex he put a finger in my butthole.

I dated a boy who wouldn't have sex with me because he was afraid of my libido. Just kidding. No one is afraid of my libido.

I dated a boy who wouldn't have sex with me because I laughed when he kissed me because he had really funny kissing technique.

I dated a boy who wouldn't have sex with me. When I broke up with him he asked for an explanation and I had to say that we were sexually incompatible. He said, "Oh."

I dated a boy who wouldn't have sex with me but he would kiss me and get me naked and hold me down and make me swear I loved him.

And I understand that the definition of the word 'love' is filled with words that also have definitions

I dated a boy who sometimes made me feel bad about myself. And not in the way where I knew he was trying to. That wouldn't've been as bad. He genuinely thought things were wrong with me.

I dated a boy whose libido I was afraid of.

I dated a boy who would invite me over to his house and then leave with friends and I would watch sports on TV with his roommate.

I dated a boy who I wasn't attracted to in even the smallest way. He got free donuts though cos he worked at this place.

I dated a boy who was so easy to manipulate that he became an appendage to me and when we broke up I experienced phantom limb syndrome instead of sadness.

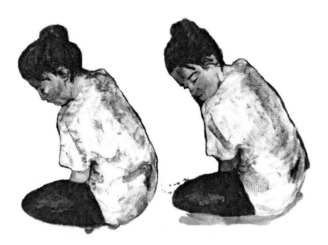

I am alone again tonight but don't worry I have this whole list of deep philosophical questions.
And if that doesn't work I will go through word documents changing periods to question marks.

20 Simple Makeup Tips for the Everyday Woman

1. When drawing on eyebrows, remember that looking mildly surprised is both sexy and fashionable.

2. Makeup should not be applied to hemorrhoids.

3. Remember: Your eyelashes are commas and boldening them does not necessarily add meaning.

4. Conceal blemishes with rhinestones for a creative edge.

5. Before you begin applying makeup, write a thesis statement and briefly outline your current purpose for using makeup and what you hope to accomplish with it.

6. In a hurry, apply liquid foundation with a ladle.

7. Stay away from reds; they'll highlight your lack thereof.

8. Gray hairs can be plucked and saved for a wig that you can use when there are no more hairs to pluck.

9. During the holiday season, double chins can be covered with a festive bow.

10. Facial tattoos should be used sparingly.

11. In a pinch, use sandpaper or pliers to add color to your cheeks.

12. You should be absolutely hairless from the mouth down.

13. Silver lipstick is always appropriate.

14. Keep your own physical faults in mind, so that you may accuse other women of having them during disagreements.

15. In the morning, pour liquid foundation into open pores. This will ensure a steady secretion of foundation all day, so that reapplication is unnecessary.

16. Try to see your face with an objective eye each day. The heavy rouge you've been sporting for five years may offend those who have not seen the historical progression.

17. Resist buying Revlon products, because their commercials suck.

18. Snort powder to make up that hard-to-reach cerebrum.

19. If your face is large, you will have to plan more makeup products into your budget.

20. Makeup can be used in large amounts and with high contrast as an alternative to hormone replacement therapy.

His Lies Taste like Eggs Benedict

You force his name casually into conversation and then you see him at Denny's. He is with his girlfriend and she is not you. She doesn't look anything like you. You worry that he had no discretion when it comes to girls. You say 'hi' like you are just friends and order coffee. He gestures to his girlfriend that he wants to leave, a touching moment. Without having been introduced to her, you ask him for his uneaten omelet and sourdough toast. This simple request suggests how comfortable you feel with him, how close and naked you had been together. His girlfriend knows this. She envisions the two of you close and naked in this way, and calculates when and where you were, how it happened, and where she had been at the time. You look at her as if to say, "I still have a pair of his boxers, but you can have them back at any time. I feel for you." She understands this, but still seems unsure about you. You would've liked to have taken her aside and explained yourself. You would've liked to have taken her aside and made jokes about his penis or cunnilingus technique. She wouldn't've laughed, though, and you wouldn't've become friends. To her, you aren't on the same team. To her, his penis and cunnilingus technique are serious matters.

He weighs his options. If he gives you the omelet, he will essentially be apologizing to you, showing that he knows you are owed something, and thereby admitting he has done something to hurt you. Denying you the omelet, on the other hand, would simply be passive aggression, which he should know is never attractive or clever. You would probably take the omelet anyway, after he left, he knew. Still, the decision is his. The omelet waits. You sip coffee, scorching hot, and don't flinch.

God's Girlfriend

God's girlfriend was on the toilet feeling more important than God, but irritable and crampy. Pissed off at the world.

What a crummy world, she thought, *God can't do anything right.*

God was in the other room, fighting with the fax machine.

Forever is so long, she thought, *You have to think about it only in smaller parts, month by month, week by week. I look forward to Thursday, when my period ends.*

I need some excitement, she thought, *God should've invented more hot guys. He probably thinks this is funny.*

She knew what was happening. She was taking the biggest crap of her life. She was embarrassed by the size of it.

"God, if this shit was a dick, that dick would be a big dick," she said.

"What?" said God.

"'What' what?" said God's girlfriend.

God said "bullshit" at the fax machine.

"It's fucking brand new," he said.

Later that evening, God's girlfriend called her mother, and they talked about how to prepare frozen meals so that they taste homemade, and they both sighed audibly.

I've been sitting in this goddamned bathroom for over an hour trying to think of a way to steal a roll of toilet paper.

Beginnings That Lead to Middles

I met JR for the first time outside of Mervyn's and we immediately got into a power struggle. He stood idly beside me, waiting for me to solicit him. I smoked my cigarette confidently two yards away, waiting to be solicited. The way I saw it was; if I had to end up being submissive and attentive to him, he should be able to grow some balls and initiate the encounter. I shouldn't have had to eagerly offer my passivity. But these, admittedly, were not the kinds of opinions that made me a successful businesswoman.

He finally said, "I'm giving you fifty dollars because that's what I want to spend, not because that's what you're charging."

I said, "If you want that much control, you can suck your own dick."

He said, "I'll give you fifty dollars to pretend you love me."

I said, "Okay, you've got one hour."

I wrapped my arms around him and said, "I love you."

He said, "Elaborate on that."

So I baked him a cherry walnut tart and sprinkled powdered sugar onto it.

He said, "Be more realistic."

So I didn't eat my portion and looked longingly into his eyes. I initiated a game of footsie that apparently made JR think our relationship was getting too complicated.

He said, "I want a kind of love that's open and comfortable."

So I told him about all the insecurities and body image issues I had as a young girl and how I dealt with those issues by running away from home. Then I fell asleep in his arms.

He said, "Well maybe I didn't mean that."

So I laughed at whatever he said. I laughed so hard I started crying, so I excused myself to the ladies' room and applied more makeup.

He said, "Someone as beautiful as you could never really love me."

So I smudged my makeup a little to make him more comfortable.

He said, "This all seems too painless to be real love."

So I stood up and demanded to know why he was home so late the night before.

He said, "I like where this is going."

So I made jealous comments about his ex-girlfriends and demanded that he reenact our first telephone conversation. When he couldn't remember the correct sequence of our conversation, I accused him of cheating on me. I ordered a bouquet of flowers online, had them delivered to myself, and made JR believe they were from another man.

He said, "I think I'm really starting to fall for you."

So I got drunk and hacked into his email account and got upset about year-old emails from other girls and then cried myself to sleep.

He said, "Now I feel left out."

So I begged him never to leave me.

He said, "Just a little less desperate and a little more playful."

So I tattooed his name onto my right breast and posted a photo of it on the Internet.

He said, "That would work really well as an action shot, don't you think?"

So I let him suckle my nipple for the last two minutes while I uploaded the new picture. I titled it 'Please don't let this end so it can never begin again.'

He said, "Can I see you again? Can I call you?" and discreetly put fifty dollars on the table. I pretended not to notice what he did.

I looked at him as if to say, "Where's my cash?"

He waited for me to pick the money up. The way I saw it was; I'm his employee, and he's my boss. I shouldn't have to remind him to pay me. He shouldn't be able to be so indirect. He gestured subtly toward the money, and I was careful not to follow his gaze. I wasn't going to let him win that easily.

Maybe Her Pending Corpse is a Window

Kate is dying. She is getting close to death. Her houseguest, an Internet stranger named Ira, who has arranged to sleep on her couch for the next four days through an online social network catering to travelers, is halfway on the sidewalk and halfway on the street in a strange town, and he is watching her die.

"Kate," he thinks, but then his thought just ends. They met less than an hour ago. They were on bicycles. He thinks this is just perfect.

He doesn't know much about her. They had dropped his things off at her apartment and were on their way to get a few groceries. He is traveling through the states. He has recently been dumped by a girlfriend and is determined to find himself. He sublet his apartment in Detroit to a couple of his ex-girlfriend's close friends. He wonders now if that was a good idea.

It is a powerful image for Ira, Kate lying here, her unfamiliar stomach fat drooping over her pants unpleasantly. It's like live reality television.

Kate's apartment was messy when they stopped in. Things were dirty, and the place had a certain monotonous quality. The couch appeared to be woven with itchy synthetics, had a sick-looking orange cat sitting on it, and was generally unappealing.

Kate's voice, if he can recall, is deep but cheerful. She's friendly and enthusiastic, but entirely unattractive. Her face is too complex to be beautiful. The lines around her nose and between her eyebrows are deep and unmistakable. When they met, he immediately abandoned the sexual agenda he had been, in three short emails, pretending not to have, and began hoping that she hadn't had one. It's supposed to be innocent, travelers helping travelers. But Ira hasn't had sex in four months and to him, everyone was a possibility.

He tries to look helpful. He uses his cell phone. He waves down drivers. His efforts are dutiful and attentive. There are no frantic memories flashing through his mind, and he gives no passionate cries for help. He is thinking clearly and is satisfied with himself for that.

Kate's blood is on the ground. It is moving in circles.

"It isn't possible to live without blood," Ira thinks.

He has never hugged her, so it doesn't occur to him that this is the same blood that would've made any such hugs warm. As Kate moves closer to death, Ira feels himself becoming alone and stranded, sees himself standing on the black concrete uselessly, a lone parasite that has found himself without a host, staring blankly at the pending corpse of what was once an abstract sexual fantasy. He sees the thoughts in his head as if they were lines of an instant message:

(3:46pm)Does the world know it doesn't need me?

(3:46pm)It does, it definitely does.

(3:46pm)Maybe the world needs me. It's possible, I think. Is it?

(3:47pm)It doesn't. It's not. No.

He briefly wonders if it would be appropriate to get the keys from her pocket and go back to her apartment once the paramedics get here and take her away with them. Keep to the itinerary despite the unexpected tragedy. But Kate has a roommate, Ira knows, and he wouldn't want to have to explain anything to her. The roommate would be overemotional and cry, probably. She would be confused and unsure about Ira sleeping there and distressed by his graphic and technical account of the accident. She would silently disapprove when he decided to sleep on her bed instead of the couch.

Kate's fingers shakily form a fist and then uncurl.

"Was that it?" Ira thinks, but he sees that she is still breathing, gently and sporadically

WHAT'S THE POINT OF HAVING SEX ORGANS WHEN MY MAIN PURPOSE IN LIFE IS TO WRITE UNEMOTIONAL POEMS USING FULL SENTENCES?

Until Whatever 23

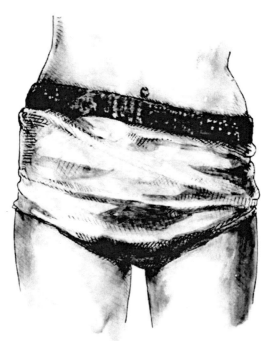

she's articulate

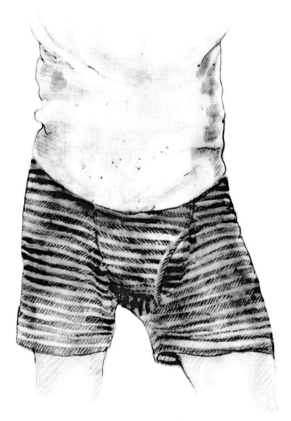

he's profound

Lets get deeply
moved

I know what you're thinking. You're thinking I shouldn't work in customer service.

I'm at the point in my life where I wake up in the morning and literally don't know what to do.

My mom says this feeling is my hormones telling me to have children, but it feels more like my hormones telling me to buy the Goosebumps series books on eBay.

The most emotional sexual experience I ever had involved a hallucination of someone I loved being in the same room while I gave someone else I loved a handjob.

But that seems strange because I'm pretty sure I've never loved anyone.

I'm at the point in my life where I masturbate to memories of cuddling.

My mom says there are some things she really doesn't need to know.

I hope it's okay that I'm not referring to all the text messages I've received while writing this.

I try to drink coffee and look out of windows but eventually I have to crap or blink.

I grew up poor and everyone who grew up poor has a somewhat decent sense of humor.

I have complex fears stemming from childhood that I don't want to talk about right now.

When I was twelve someone bought me a case of SoBe and I felt rich and powerful. Ever since then my sense of humor has been confusing and aggressive.

Now I'm writing poetry because I'm beginning to feel serious about life.

Serious like *if I don't write poetry right now, someone is going to make me do the dishes.*

Or *if I don't write poetry right now, someone is going to tell me about their day.*

All I did was compliment someone's jacket and it somehow turned into a two-minute conversation where I had to say *happy birthday* at the end. I don't know how these things happen to me.

Nothing Can Make Me Feel Sincere Not Even True Love.

Not even love and not even MTV's True Life.

I want to be in love but how can I.

I can't even write a love poem without referring to MTV or Lord of the Rings or something. Plus everyone I know is in love with me a little which makes it hard to think anyone is special.

I just want to wake up in the morning and feel like someone is planning on seeing me.

And I want to like myself through someone else instead of just me all the time.

This is about as sincere as I could possibly be. And it sounds boring and self-assured.

I just want everyone to think I'm on my way to Burger King.

It Could've Been a Photograph of Anybody.

I created an indentation in my bed where I always sit and write. I think of this indentation as concrete proof that I've existed the last several months. It feels like a photograph of myself, but not exactly.

It makes me feel present, but not entirely.

It makes me feel like I'm sitting on a bench with someone I love and we're holding hands in a strange way where all our fingertips align and we're talking about a party we might go to and we're making out a little and I feel kind of bad because I've just stolen a lot of cardstock from an art store that I respect.

EVERYONE THINKS I'M BRILLIANT —AND I AM—BUT I'M ALSO MODEST.

I'm Not Drunk, I'm Big-Boned.

I want to erase everything I've ever written and go rent videos but I can't because I don't know what videos to rent.

I am letting myself feel detached right now.

I am always trying to sabotage my own work.

I want to end this, but I haven't said anything tangible about myself yet.

Okay here is my phone number 707-888-1744.

I write poetry because if I don't I will have to think about serious things.

I used to run track but then I got boobs and couldn't run because I was very busy buying bras and crying about stretch marks.

But now I have had boobs for eight years and I barely have time to think about them anymore.

Yes, do the math.

I am writing poetry right now so that I can pretend I don't hear someone doing the dishes.

I used to clean the neighbor's house for money and she had a vending machine in her garage.

I used to make a magazine about wildlife and I sold a subscription to my neighbor but I got tired of making it so I just cut up parts of Ranger Rick and pasted them onto folded printer paper.

Now I have boobs though. Things are different.

Are you really still doing the math about my boobs?

Maybe I'm laughing while I write this because I have no capacity to take anything seriously.

I like poetry because it feels like television. Good poetry feels good like television.

I think it's really funny to call someone *the history channel* but I've used this joke a lot of times and no one has ever laughed.

No, I'm lying.

When I said no I meant yes and when I said lying I meant ovulating.

This is what I mean by poetry.

My mom is at her house waiting for this poem to earn me some money.

We love each other because we look like each other.

I never take myself seriously because I'm not boring enough.

But I am boring enough to sit at a computer for hours typing out explanations of myself.

I SHOULD MEASURE MY HEARTBEAT OR SOMETHING.

Even on Christmas I try to be in a text message conversation at all times.

Christmas trees can be enjoyed for about one day and after that it feels like someone is on their way over to cross their hands over their crossed knees and look at you expecting answers.

One day I will be a supportive friend but for now I'm still playing with the poetry refrigerator magnets.

Alone please, and yes I've heard of exquisite corpse.

I'm making it seem like I don't like my friends but I don't like anything except photographs of orphans.

My mom wants me home for Christmas but I want it to be my idea.

I want everyone to read this poem and say *I bet her tits are real*.

I have started a band and my gimmick is I only write songs about the neighbor's dog and pretend to be displacing my emotions.

Once I overheard my mom telling my aunt that I was a mistake and I revealed myself from the Lego castle I was crouched behind and told her what I'd heard and she said, "What do you want, I'm only five or six years older than you."

I will listen to hours and hours of insignificant rambling if you want, but I won't stop rubbing my mustache until you tell me how you feel about me and my mustache.

I have collection agencies fighting for my attention. Where is my minivan? I just found rockstar parking. Please call Geico and tell them I've found someone else. Tell the paparazzi I am in parking section G4 and that I'm picking my camel toe.

I could be charming and sociable if I wanted but then I wouldn't be mysterious anymore and anyway I'm too busy with my band.

I've been asked to write inspirational slash instrumental music for a colon hydrotherapy clinic and I will be getting paid in paper pillowcases and paper bed sheets.

Is Everyone Ready to See My Muscles?

Sometimes when I think I'm in love I think, "Wait, no I'm not."

It seems that I have gotten carried away with my own ridiculous projections of who the person is. No one can fulfill my projections. That's just science.

Anyways, people only love each other so they can complain about each other.

I asked my mom straight up, "What is it exactly that you like about my paternal uncle, who you have been dating for five years, since around the time I first met my dad and he introduced us to his brother, my uncle, your boyfriend?"

I'm a strong and independent woman, not a dyke.

I'm confused about my sexuality, not my sexual orientation.

As in, *is this my labia minora? It seems big.*

Or *should I be running out of lube this quickly?*

My left arm is asleep but I am moving forward with this poem anyway.

Can I carry your children for money?

Would you like to harvest my eggs for money?

Or do you need a babysitter?

EVERYONE TOLD ME I LOOKED DIFFERENT TODAY. MY MOM SAID THIS IS BECAUSE MAYBE I'M OVULATING.
SHE SAID MAYBE I'M EITHER HAPPY OR OVULATING.

The moral of the story is, do you think I'm fat?

I want to know everything you know about me, what does it mean that I talk the way I talk, does that affect you, I'm serious, I'm honest, I'm *that* selfish, I'm really curious about this.

You always tell me who I am, I like that, it makes me like you, I want to be more like what I seem like to you, I like that version of me, it makes me be able to stand you.

Let's talk about my feelings and then your feelings about me.

I used to like small glass figurines, I collected them, it got a little out of control, I ran out of places to display them, does that give you any insight here?

I want to own you and take you far away where we can embarrass each other in public, I like you, you are impossible, you are insane, this is crazy, be my husband, I want anything, we will die before anyone realizes we're joking, did I just say 'we' I meant 'me me me.'

I'm busy tonight, how about tomorrow, I only really like you for your body anyway, it is so fucked up, hilarious, I want you under my covers with me far away thinking about you, I love you, let's talk to each other using only allegories, let's shake hands, please shake my hand, let's be married and hate each other, let's move away just to make our friends sad. I want us to be sad forever together and be miserably celibate out of an inability to speak to each other in ways that don't turn us both off.

I want to text message my mom something cute like *I met a boy*, which is why I'm wearing makeup today.

I am feeling like myself, which feels like I can say anything I want. It feels like I'm not even watching myself on a television screen just above your head. And I'm talking in a way that sounds like I think no one else is around to hear me.

Watch this. I can make fun of myself in a way that makes you feel bad about yourself and I can do this and make you think I'm insecure at the same time and you will think it's totally charming.

Let me guess. You want to get a drink with me sometime. Just kidding. I don't have a boyfriend. I just wanted to see if you'd believe me.

If I rest the weight of my upper body on this rail you will think I am either sick of talking to you or trying to show you my boobs. And that is exactly the kind of tension we need to move this relationship forward.

By *move this relationship forward* I mean *give me your phone number and I will probably not call you*.

By *probably* I mean *drunkenly*.

And by *phone number* I mean *expensive jewelry*.

I don't think you'd like me on many other days. I know I am sarcastic and accommodating, but I am also small and quiet and won't like you very much or very often.

I'm not mad. I just can't find my cell phone to pretend I have a call.

ovulatin'

I bought some pills, morning after pills, to plant
in my purse so that one day they might spill out
and someone might see them and believe, however
briefly, that I was having sex or even had a
boyfriend.

What Are You Wearing!

There were three boys: Damien, Nick, and Raphael.

Tanya said, "Let me see here." And then, "Who has the nicest hair?"

Raphael raised a hand. It was clear that he did have the nicest hair.

Tanya said, "Who is the most attractive in general?"

Raphael said, "Me, again."

No one considered disputing this, either.

Nick said, "Ask something about being funny."

Damien said, "Or about emotional availability."

Tanya said, "Are any of you single?"

Raphael said, "I'm not sure what you mean."

Nick said, "I'm only one person, yes."

Damien said, "Could you repeat that?"

Tanya said, "Um." And then, "Yeah."

When she was fourteen, Tanya cut her hair into a boy's bob, and her grandma stopped loving her until it grew past her ears. They called her into the principal's office the day it happened, to tell her that her grandma could finally love her again, and that she could go home early. On the way home she saw a mountain lion sleeping with dried weeds tangled in his whiskers.

Tanya turned around and said, "What color are my eyes?"

Damien said, "Green."

Raphael said, "Grey."

Nick said, "What difference does it make?"

Fable

Maya was a startlingly beautiful girl, and for this reason had trouble making female friends. Often, out of desperation, Maya phoned her mother, Catherine, to gush about her current love interests.

"Just make sure you get tested regularly," Catherine would say, for though she was deeply disturbed by her daughter's sexual candidness, she understood the root of Maya's social inadequacies, and wanted her to feel as normal as possible.

Angela was one of those girls who knew the shoe size of every guy on the lacrosse team, including Coach Feseden, who wore embarrassingly unfashionable Keds and purposely ordered the cheerleader's skirts one size too small. Angela teased and manipulated Maya with hyper girl talk between classes.

"Coach Feseden is sooo cute, don't you think, Maya?"

Maya, wanting terribly to be invited to Angela's Sweet Sixteen party, agreed, and soon developed a crush on Coach Feseden.

For a long time, no one knew where Coach Feseden took Maya. Catherine went on prime-time television begging America for help in finding her. After a few months, everyone assumed he had left the country and that there was nothing they could do. Catherine suffered and, being the only active psychiatrist in the Tristate area, refused her services to everyone, even the psychologically neediest.

People self-medicated. They lost their jobs. Suicide rates skyrocketed. Organic products were rotting on the shelves because everyone was too depressed to care about their health anymore. They begged Catherine to analyze their psyches, to prescribe just one little teeny insignificant bottle of Seroquel®, but she wouldn't.

"If I must suffer then everyone must suffer," she said, and made funny faces at a nearby baby.

Deer Grazing

You're standing in front of a painting of two deer
grazing. You're at home. This painting belongs to
you. You see yourself in the deer. You see yourself as
one of two. You notice that one of the deer seems to
be trying to impress the other deer by grazing in a
very sexual manner. You think that this must be the
deer that represents your boyfriend; he would totally
try to have sex during a meal. "Hahaha," you think
to yourself. The other deer isn't eating, her chin is
just resting on the ground. You would think she was
eating unless you looked really carefully, like you are
now. And actually, you realize, upon noticing how
wide and vacant her eyes are, how shiny and glazed
they are; she's stuffed. A hidden pin holds up her tail.
Her fur has clearly been airbrushed, the natural color
long faded away. She's been dead for a long time and
no one seems to notice. You remember you need to buy
makeup.

Your Only Memory of Him

Your shirt was off and he was smelling the area
between your breasts. As he moves his head, the area
gets larger and larger until your breasts are at least
a mile away from each other and he has fallen asleep
between them.

I will wrangle your turd for two small payments of
$59.99
and and I will throw in two free lemon zesters.

Things I Know About Men

Nobody teaches men 'the sooner the better' in terms of when to ask you to take off your top. Everybody thinks they'll just learn that on their own, I guess. Men also drive cars sometimes.

Things I Know About Egg Donation

Parents, when given the option, choose egg donors with long legs and big tits.

Things I Know About Alcohol

Alcohol is a tool of self-discovery. Drink four shots to see into the future. Drink five shots to heighten your sense of gravity. Drink six shots to double your chances of conception. Drink seven shots to undo the past. Drink eight shots to develop healthy sleep patterns.

Things I Know About Condoms

What do you do with a box of 50,000 condoms? Put the box by your bed and when people come over and look inquisitively into the box, make an exhausted, dreamy expression.

Held Together Wrists

He came over and we studied my water purifier together.

"It looks like it needs a new filter," he said.

"But I love this filter," I said. "Sometimes I think it's the only thing in my life that's consistent."

We drank water and I tried to think of a way to make him hold my wrists together without asking him to do it. Usually, if he was around, especially if I was fully awake, I was trying to make him hold my wrists together without telling him to do it. It hadn't ever worked. It's just that it wouldn't've been special if I had to tell him to do it.

"Why don't you ever use my name in the stories you write about me?" he said.

"I use your name all the time," I said, "I'm using it right now."

For twenty dollars, I could buy a new filter. But for forty dollars, I could buy a whole new water purifying system and turn the whole world upside down.

"What do you think of that?" I said.

"I don't know if a new water purifying system will change your life that dramatically."

"It's not important that there's drama," I said, crying, having poked myself in the eye while gesturing for dramatic effect.

We didn't used to fight like this. Or try to change each other's minds. I didn't used to write stories about small things without trying to make them seem significant. But we were in a national economic crisis and things had changed, yes.

I, for one, had changed.

"I wish I was rich," I said, "Or in love. Rich or in love."

"I hope you're not trying to start a conversation about the economic crisis," he said. I saw him looking at my wrists and got a hopeful feeling. There was something beautiful about him that I couldn't quite put to words. Something about the crevices in his face made me believe I could be a good stage-makeup artist.

"I will buy you this filter," he said, "If you'll pretend we don't know each other at the cash register."

I'm writing about love because no one else ever has and because I'm wearing jeans that make my butt look good.

I have this friend who has this boyfriend who isn't really a boyfriend but he emotionally abuses her, I heard. He figures out what she's insecure about and then gives her really transparent compliments that make her feel bad about her personality. She tries to pretend her feelings are hurt. I used to think the adjective a person uses the most often is the word that most accurately describes what kind of person they are. But this friend never uses the word 'submissive.'

They have a date one night, and my friend finally gets up the courage to tell him how much she loves him, but before she can say anything he goes, "Have you ever been in love?"

And she says, "No, I don't know. Yeah. I don't know. No."

And he's like, "I have. It's really great. You should be in love. Only not with me. You shouldn't fall in love with me. I have a lot of very lovable friends I could introduce you to, though."

And she goes, "It's okay,"

And he says, "Being in love is really great, I think. You should be in love. You should try it."

And she says, "I don't think we should talk about love."

And he says, "Why? It doesn't matter. I was in love with this girl and we dated for three years but it was on and off so it was funner that way."

And she's like, "Cool."

And he says, "That was pretty condescending."

And she says, "How old are you?"

And he says, "Twenty-one."

And she says, "I'm twenty-two."

Even an idiot could wake up in the morning and eat his groceries and earn money and figure out what was wrong with his life and still have time to be a normal, excitable, somewhat apprehensive boyfriend.

But this idiot isn't a boyfriend.

A boyfriend would want to spend the night.

After the date my friend called me sounding bored and exhausted.

"Today I had a date and my date fell asleep during the date," she said.

"Is that what the entire date consisted of?" I asked.

"No," she said, "but that's the only part worth talking about."

What you do

	DRINK	ABSTAIN
DRINK	Highest chance of Sexual encounter	Highest chance of Me embarrassing myself
ABSTAIN	I can enjoy your uninhibitedness w/o endangering my own social standing	We must rely on social adequacy & conversation skills to forward our relationship

what I do

Aftermath of the 90's

You send him a text message explaining why you are sending him a text message. "Yr famous," it says, "want 2 hang out?" He texts you back hours later while you are stealing fountain soda from a Burger King, "Ya OK. Want 2 steal salads from Sizzler or something l8r?" This sophisticated choice in restaurant makes you worry about your class differences, but you meet him at Sizzler and hope there isn't a theft protection device on the salad bar. You share a plate of pickled beets and chicken wings on the curb three blocks away and have a conversation about music that you only barely have a grasp on. He tries to convince you that something something contemporary alternative something easily applies to rock theory, something something something. You hold firm ground against this concept, and he affectionately calls you old fashioned. You kiss with greasy chicken wing lips and hold hands back to your bicycles, where you exchange chicken salts once more and ride off separately, not looking back.

Telescope

My dad bought a telescope as a prelude to the sex talk he would give me the next month.

"This is Saturn," he said. "And here is a small star."

He said I could point the telescope at whatever star I wanted. I said he could go ahead, and that I didn't care very much what we looked at.

"Me and your mother used to go to the park at night and look at the sky together."

"Look, that star looks kind of bluish." I tried to point the telescope in the direction of the bluish star, but aiming a telescope is pretty hard.

"Should we stay out here much longer?" I asked. I wanted dinner.

My dad looked at me in a way I understood to be meaningful. He was forcing a moment. But I knew that, as an eleven-year-old girl, I was not responsible to figure out what the subtext was. I suppose my dad was always trying to tell me how sad he was inside.

"It's just that I'm hungry," I said.

My diary used to be filled with positive body image affirmations, but now it is filled with anxiety about debt and weekly observations of this weird mole I have.

Until Whatever   55

WTF QT Sup

He spelled his own name incorrectly, P-o-l, and said, "That's the way I pronounce it." It didn't match his identification card, I told him, and his paperwork was probably going to get lost.

"My paperwork," he said, "is inconsequential. I'm here to get my nipples pierced." His attitude earned him some deliberately lost paperwork. I called him up to the counter to give him some new questionnaires to fill out. And a dried out pen.

"I see my forms right there under that Chinese take out box," he said. I told him that this was a common occurrence, that we can't always keep track of paperwork that is filled out inaccurately, and to try not to take it personally. Sometimes these things just get lost in the system. We'd be with him as soon as he turned in the new completed forms.

When he took his seat, I looked over his original paperwork. Pol Few, 32 years old, male. He even sounded hot on paper.

The chief body piercer, Stan, came to the front desk and asked if there were any appointments, and I said no, not at the moment. I said if he wanted to, he could go grab lunch or run an errand while things were slow.

I watched Pol scribble on his questionnaire, trying to get his pen to work. He had the body type I'm usually attracted to, not fat or muscular, but round, and taut.

Pol came up to the desk and handed me his new paperwork. He asked me when he could expect to be seen and I explained that the chief body piercer had an emergency to attend to, but should be back shortly. I asked that he please bear with us so that we may pierce his nipples with the care and efficiency we are reputed for.

Pol flipped through a tattoo design magazine. I stared at his reflection on my computer screen, imagining my body parts in his. Lips in nostrils, feet between buttocks, neck between thighs, slippery mouth in crook of neck.

My biggest problem was that I could make mistakes over and over for years and still not ever figure out what I've figured out. My other biggest problem was that I hadn't been naked with a man in over ten months. A lot can happen in ten months. New underwear had been bought, gotten old, and been thrown away during that time. The exact length of my pubic hair began to seem trivial. My friends suddenly felt they had the right to be surprised and upset if I didn't return their phone calls within eight hours. My mom asked me if I was a lesbian. My condoms expired. I started watching David Letterman every night and then had to watch it just to get to sleep. I finally found a florist I liked and she died. I read the Diary of Anne Frank and got upset. I completely forgot about my phone bill for five months and then remembered and paid it and didn't feel different in any way about anything.

The Protagonist

Recently, I saw a movie about a protagonist and her love interest who is perfect for her in every way, but who she is destined never to meet. Viewers go back and forth between the protagonist's painfully lonely life and her love interest's equally depressing and pointless existence. In one scene, we see a close-up of the protagonist as she moves her lips around for an extended amount of time, as if searching the alphabet for a letter that feels like it will begin the sentence she wants to say but doesn't quite have the words for.

Then she says, "Pepperoni," and someone hands her a slice of pizza.

The general sense I got from the movie is that life is futile.

About halfway through the movie, the love interest is completely dropped from the film with no explanation.

The protagonist ends up with someone who thinks she's really hot.

TIRED OF WASTING MONEY
BY EATING HEALTH FOODS?
THAT'S A PROBLEM!

TOO MANY BILLS? SUICIDE!

HAVING A TOUGH TIME
FINDING A DATE? WE CARE!

LIKE WHAT YOU SEE? EMAIL
MY COUSIN HELENA—WE
HAVE SIMILAR BONE
STRUCTURE!

DEPRESSED AND/OR UGLY?
HMM! WE DON'T KNOW!

EDIBLE UNDIES STUCK IN
HAIR DRYER? YOU MUST
HAVE A COOL LIFE!

TROUBLE GRASPING
INFINTY? WHAT DO YOU
WANT ME TO SAY!

COLLEGE GRADUATE? JOIN THE MILLIONS JUST LIKE YOU!

SUICIDAL? SORRY, I CAN'T HEAR YOU—I'M GOING DOWN A WATER SLIDE!

IDENTITY CRISIS? WHAT'S UP!

DRUNK? DO SOME TEXT MESSAGING!

DREAMT OF LITTLE ALIENS RUMMAGING THROUGH YOUR TRASH WHILE YOUR SISTER MORPHED INTO A SNAIL CREATURE? THAT'S SO INTERESTING—CAN YOU TELL ME THAT STORY AGAIN!

Manipulation, Energy Drinks, and Time Travel

Seriously, I will become a TV executive just for you. I'll buy up all the television stations and make sure my executives only hire program managers who only hire casting directors that only cast moderately attractive girls. We'll make the moderately attractive girls famous, me and my crew. You'll never see a girl on TV prettier than me.

I'll buy chocolate covered cherries and drop them into your mouth from skyscrapers as you unknowingly walk by. I'll put my name on them somehow, so you know they're from me. I'll teach you Braille. Tongue Braille.

I'll be yours forever. I won't even look at other guys. I won't answer their phone calls even if they're business related. I won't manipulate them. Unless you want me to. I can treat guys badly for your entertainment. I will lead them on for months, answering their text messages using an increasingly sexy vocabulary. I will call them 'Beast' in private and then, at a time you determine is right, I will humiliate them irrevocably. I will laugh at their serious comment about how they feel about me, mispronounce their name, and then the people from *What Not To Wear* will come in and ask if they want to be on *What Not To Wear*. I will coordinate it so that the people from *What Not To Wear* come in at the right time. I'll record the event with my personal video camera so the video editors from *What Not To Wear* will have more humiliating footage to choose from.

I can manipulate guys more subtly, if you're not into reality TV and everything. I can say like, "Eee-yeahhh," after they say something, like people do. I can be condescending. I can breathe in deeply and raise my eyebrows while they talk to me.

I'll cancel Netflix, I don't know why, but I swear to god I'll do it.

Problems

Among other things, Jessica knew the names of all her friends by heart. She knew when to use nicknames and when not to. She knew how important the difference was.

Whenever she had a kitten she ignored it. She didn't want to get too attached to its cute kitten form. By the time it became a cat she had completely abandoned the idea of ever being close to it.

Jessica let her friends know things about her personal life. She told people when she felt drunk, for instance, if there were people around and it was appropriate to say such a thing.

She wanted to write an email to someone she once knew. She wanted the email to say just his name, and nothing else. She thought she would become very emotional if she ever received an email from him with just her name in it. It seemed so powerful.

She just wanted him to know she still thought about him and thought about his name.

There were things she had said to him that she had never said to anyone else. There was a time she let him express how strongly he felt for her over the phone while she remained silent. He had never done that before.

"I have a boyfriend," she said finally.

"You didn't tell me," he said.

And she called him again a few months later, but it wasn't the same.

Jessica pronounced words very lazily. She had other bad habits. She misused words. She threw around compliments. She whispered her name when introducing herself to people. She treated people badly if they were expecting her to. She didn't know how to be close to felines, but we already went over this.

She called her friends on the phone at night and asked if they would talk about themselves until she fell asleep.

I ACCIDENTALLY SHAT ON A PERSON ONCE. THERE, I SAID IT.

Girls' Guide to Boyfriends in Bathrooms

You are in the bathtub, lying opposite one another. You start slipping down into the water, but you are stopped, vaginally, by your boyfriend's foot. You realize this is the first opportunity you have ever had to pee on his foot without him noticing.

I think it's sad that they only sell the kind of shirts I like at Disneyland.

I think it's sad that they're making me work on Christmas.

And that all the other states seem so far away from California.

And that no one has ever heard of Wyoming.

And that fingernails don't grow in vibrant colors.

I $ You

1. Buy artificial inseminations for you and your four closest girl friends. Make sure the sperm donor is the same for all five of you. Remain friends throughout your pregnancies and your children's lives. Decide whose kid is best.

2. Legally adopt your brother's child. Live with him and help raise the child. Explain to others how that isn't incest.

3. Have a kid and don't name it. On its fifth birthday, let it pick out its own name. Save money by insisting that the privilege of naming oneself is a valuable gift.

4. Gather five good boyfriends. Have sex with each of them until you get pregnant. After childbirth, give the baby a paternity test. Marry the biological father.

5. Get artificially inseminated by your brother. Explain to others how that isn't incest.

6. Get pregnant with your boyfriend. Simultaneously, hire a surrogate mother to carry a baby made with your egg and your boyfriend's sperm. See which baby turns out cuter.

7. Donate your eggs to curb the costs of all your abortions.

8. Tell your kid about blow jobs before you tell them about sex.

9. Be the surrogate mother for your grandparents. Abort the baby at the last minute.

10. Play a Russian Roulette Pregnancy: Get five sperm donors, only one of which is a desirable candidate for a biological father, and toss their sperm donation cylinders in a top hat. Choose one randomly. After childbirth, try to figure out whose baby you have.

11. Pretend you're a prostitute but only have sex with one customer. Once you're pregnant, sue for child support.

12. Get artificially inseminated by a ten-year-old. Explain to others why that isn't pedophilia.

13. Get artificially inseminated by your son. Name the resulting baby after yourself.

14. Tell people you're 'pro-abortion', not 'pro-choice'.

15. Get pregnant at the same time as your sister. After childbirth, switch kids. Switch back when they're five. Ask them if they missed you.

16. When you're fifteen, get pregnant and then sue your parents for not explaining sex to you.

17. Get famous. Donate your eggs and see who notices their kids' resemblance to you.

18. Get pregnant and go to an abortion clinic. Allow yourself to be persuaded to keep the baby. Demand child support from the pro-life activists.

19. You and your boyfriend get two sets of clones. When the clones are old enough, tell them each to reproduce. See if the offspring is identical.

20. Leave your baby at the hospital.

21. Cry loudly at your mom's funeral until someone agrees to adopt you.

22. Marry someone with the same last name as you. Go through the name-changing paperwork anyway.

23. Give your kids legal first names that are traditionally nicknames: Rob, Billy, and Becky.

24. Get pregnant. Artificially inseminate the growing baby inside of you.

25. Be the surrogate mother for your best friend's baby, and she for yours. After both childbirths, determine which baby you're most drawn to emotionally.

26. When your friend is drunk and blacked out, get her artificially inseminated. Don't tell her.

27. Give abortion coupons to your friend as a baby shower gift. Say, "Preparation is key."

28. Put your baby up for adoption. Ten years later, marry the baby's adoptive father. Act like a step-mom.

29. Fill your daughter's hope chest with condoms, makeup and morning-after pills.

30. Encourage your sister to get artificially inseminated by someone hotter than her husband.

31. Convince your sister to let you get artificially inseminated by her husband.

32. Cheat on your husband with your marriage counselor.

33. Make a few clones of yourself, simultaneously. Hire illegal immigrants to be the surrogate mothers. Die before the childbirths.

34. Be the surrogate mother for an awful ex-boyfriend's clone. Give the clone Fetal Alcohol Syndrome.

35. Fall asleep during sex. Sue your husband for raping you.

36. Choose a sperm donor who maintains an afro.

37. Ask your child to pick its favorite parent.

38. For your daughter's twelfth birthday, buy her a mood ring and sausage flavored condoms.

39. Take photographs of your miscarriages. Put each of them in a scrapbook next to the photographs of the objects or people that you suspect caused the miscarriage.

40. Allow a homeless man to impregnate you. Insist that he have partial custody of the resulting child.

Kurt and Courtney

I realized I was in love with Andrew after I saw him shirtless at the 2nd Annual Kurt & Courtney themed Pool Party. He had a wet thermal tied around his waste and smudged lipstick and he smoked a cigarette melodramatically, but I saw him touch his chubby stomach insecurely, and suddenly I wanted to protect him. His stomach seemed inviting, like I was invited. The drug jokes got boring and everyone started talking sarcastically about Pro Wrestling. At one point, at the punch bowl, I said to Andrew "I love you," and he said "I love you, too," and we walked away from each other.

I was drunk and threw a pool toy from too far away from the pool and it hit the foot of a girl who was sitting at the edge of the pool. She swore at me belligerently and Andrew suggested I be more careful. He said it nicely and in-character but I suffered internally for the next hour, which probably helped my costume. He didn't deserve me. All the Courtney's wore their ripped fishnets into the pool and threw their blonde wigs at each other and Andrew was in love with all of them but me. I wanted to kill myself so I did, with a water gun full of vodka straight into the mouth.

Aphorism

There are no 'right' answers, just long boring ones and short funny ones.

Life is Time Consuming

My friend Andy always makes jokes about being in love with me. I think he jokes about it too much for it to be a joke.

I just called Verizon Wireless Customer Service and flirted with the Customer Service Representative and he quickly transferred me to a female Customer Service Representative, and I was very polite to her even though I felt humiliated.

I've been sending emails to this guy I used to babysit. He seems interested in the garage punk rock 60s Beatles scene, which I find really surprising.

My friend Dane comes over and we talk about math because he studies math. In my head I always exchange the math words for sex words, but I don't think he gets it. He just thinks I don't know what I'm talking about. I'm trying to find a way to make a sexually suggestive diagram for him for Valentine's Day, not that I'm interested.

I just checked out the mailman. We just made eye contact. Oh shit, I think he's coming over here to deliver a package.

My friend Ked buys me any food we eat when we're together. When I'm annoyed with him I insist on paying for my own food.

Sometimes on the bus I make men fall in love with me by looking out the window and thinking very unnecessary, negative things about them.

I just accidentally licked my lips while maintaining eye contact with a gentleman on a skateboard. There's a name for when that happens.

I love being happy
I love being happy, too

I'm happy
I'm happy, too

Acronyms To Expedite Conversation

BYOBF
Bring your own best friend

TIJLTEODC
This is just like that episode of Dawson's Creek

TIJLTEOF
This is just like that episode of Frasier

TIJLTMABL
This is just like that movie A Bug's Life

TIJLTMA
This is just like that movie ANTZ

DYW2DB2NOIDK
Do you want to drink beer tonight, or I don't know

FL
Fried labia

TRG
That's really great

NAJKJK
Nice ass, just kidding just kidding

LOLNL
Laughing out last night's lasagna

PT
Posh tosh

WWF
Whatever whatever forever

MMJCANIFC
My mom just called and now I feel crazy

MMJCAMMRSATE
My mom just called and made me really scared about
the economy

ISATE
I'm scared about the economy

YKWIM
You know what I mean

ITAL
I'm talking about love

TIJLTSFHM
This is just like that scene from Home Alone

TIJLIHAWKGIMMFD
This is just like in Home Alone when Kevin goes "I
made my family disappear."

IFLWHA
I feel like watching Home Alone

CSM
Communal sex mattress

RUSI
Are you sad inside

PAB
Poop ass butt

HHAYIG
Hi how are you I'm great

AW
Anyways whatever

Pfeiffer

I'm telling myself not to finish my novel until I get
some real living done. But the novel finishes itself
nightly. And I bawl to every single movie now.

My novel keeps ending in a way that I don't want,
and I have to erase it. It always ends like the movies
end. Everything comes together succinctly. In the
end of my novel, Pfeiffer comes in out of nowhere and
starts proclaiming things, starts making everyone feel
very emotional. It's hard not to feel emotional around
Pfeiffer; she's a very serious actress. But my novel is
about two people sitting on a dock eating a sandwich
together and throwing bits of sandwich into the water.
It's clear that she doesn't belong, so I take her out.

My characters never get to say what they want to
say. Pfeiffer is trying really hard to be a part of my
novel. I erase her over and over. Character One says,
"Are we trying to get the ducks to eat this?" Pfeiffer
appears and disappears. Where is she when she is
not in my novel? Character Two says, "The ducks are
insignificant. The ducks are just pretense." My characters both feel strong emotion. Character One thinks,
"Sometimes a duck eats the piece of bread, sometimes
the piece of bread just sinks." Character Two thinks,
"The other character is the most normal person I
have ever met." Pfeiffer comes in and says something
extremely quotable. My characters notice that she
has excellent posture. My characters roll their eyes. I
edit. They don't roll their eyes. I write lines about the
shape of Pfeiffer's upper lip and read them out loud.
Details are significant. I get teary-eyed over my own
writing. My characters try to figure out if the ducks
are symbolic or if the sandwich is. I erase stuff. I don't
know. I cry a little more. I have the capacity to carry

children and sometimes this causes me to act like a psychopath.

When I turn on the TV, Pfeiffer appears smiling naturally, hair bouncing. I turn the TV off and my novel loses all meaning. It would be so easy to turn the TV back on, let her tell me what I'm feeling. Because what am I feeling? But I'm scared of Pfeiffer. She can convey any emotion requested of her. My novel is in the other room and as I turn the TV off and on, the word count adjusts accordingly.

Everyone who lives in Oakland needs a shower.

Everyone who lives in San Francisco is obsessed with Frida Kahlo.

Everyone who lives in Portland is good-looking.

Everyone who lives in LA already has enough friends, thanks anyways.

Everyone who lives in Seattle walks really, really fast.

Everyone who lives in Denver lives at the airport.

Everyone who lives in Sioux Falls can tell what a chicken has eaten based on the taste and texture of its egg.

Everyone who lives in Paris has never met me.

Everyone who lives in Brooklyn is always trying to sneak the word Brooklyn into conversation.

Everyone who lives in Spokane has loyalty issues.

Everyone who lives in Austin gets aggressive when they feel vulnerable.

Everyone who lives in Copenhagen is a D-list celebrity.

Everyone who lives in New York City knows all too well to show up early to dentist appointments.

Everyone who lives in Reno chews tobacco.

Everyone who lives in Sydney clicks the who has a crush on you button on Myspace when they think no one is tracking their Internet usage.

Everyone who lives in Atlanta blasts terrible music from their crappy cars at 3am.

Everyone who lives in New Orleans costs the US government $3.00 per day somehow.

Everyone who lives in Honolulu regrets their first tattoo.

Everyone who lives in Nashville is supposed to be sending child support to my mom.

Everyone who lives in Minneapolis has an irrational fear of running into Prince at a party.

Everyone who lives in Orlando can do really good cursive uppercase 'G's.

To Do List

1. I'm making a restaurant that sells only hard-boiled eggs and I need you to create the menu.

2. I want the menu to go over, in detail, the cost of each element needed to prepare and serve a hard boiled egg, and maintain business (water, pan, electricity, chef, etc). The price of the egg will be completely rationalized and 100% accurate.

3. Then, each element in that list will be researched in the same way, each item completely rationalized in price (what the pan manufacturer needs to produce pan – metal, electricity, etc., what water company needs to maintain business – employees, energy, etc., what chef's financial needs are – food, rent, sending kids to college, etc).

4. Each element from the third list will be gone over in the same way. Do you see where this is going? Menu will be infinite.

5. This project should take your whole life to complete probably.

6. If you finish early, please check your answers.

I AM ALONE AGAIN TONIGHT BUT DON'T WORRY I AM WRITING JOKES ABOUT MY PERSONALITY.

80 Everything Was Fine

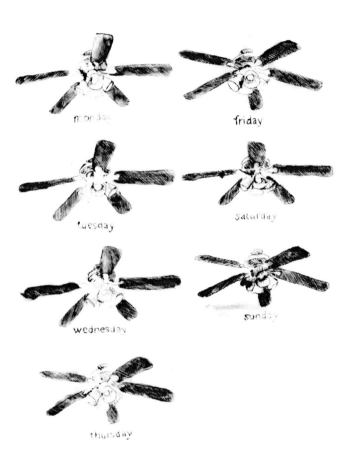

monday

friday

tuesday

saturday

wednesday

sunday

thursday

Do you want me to be sincere or do you want be to be myself?

In retrospect, yeah, I shouldn't've started fasting until after I broke up with Colt. I didn't realize fasting would make me so sweaty and introspective and emotional. I guess there wasn't much of a decision-making process. And Colt is hard to calm down anyways, once he's worked up, but every time I heard myself say something like "It's not like I stopped caring about you all of a sudden," I would get this chill all through me. I felt like I could see into my intestines. It felt like everything I said was the exact only thing to say at that moment, like my life was leading to it, and I was fulfilling all prophecies. And my sweat smelled terrible. Like insect repellent. Or horse-shoe-polish-remover-scented room-deodorizer.

"Why?" he said. I tried to allude to his insufficiencies, not spell them out.

I stayed up all night after I broke up with him, partly because I was reliving the conversation over and over and over, and partly because I couldn't sleep. My body hadn't done anything all day, hadn't stood up, hadn't worked, hadn't digested anything, had basically napped all day; wasn't tired.

Around 3am I started regretting the break up. I was getting confused. I called Colt and cried to him and sort of was out of my mind. He cried too. It was sad. I needed a shower but I was too weak. That's what I told Colt when I called him.

"Um," he said.

"What if I call you tomorrow and want to date you again?" I said. "Would that be okay or weird?"

"I don't know," he said. I was partially beginning to think that I was just breaking up with Colt out of boredom. There's a lot of extra time, suddenly, if you're not eating or preparing meals or planning them in your head or cleaning dishes or buying Tupperware.

Our collaboration was over, if you could call it that, which I suddenly felt like doing. We had been carving small animals out of wood together, so to speak, for one and a half years, but all that was over. He had asked me once to shave his initials into my pubic hair and I had outright said no. Maybe it hadn't been a joke. I was clearly the bad guy in the relationship.

I sat up in bed and got a little dizzy. I felt metaphysical and euphoric and bewildered. I couldn't remember when I had decided to break up with Colt. Maybe, I thought, it was the fast that had gotten me into this mess. But maybe, then again, who knows, maybe the fast was right after all. It kept seeming right. Like prophetic. The word 'prophetic' kept appearing in my head. I kept peeing and the pee kept being bright orange even though I was only having water.

I was alone and my body was a large part of who I was, that seemed clear, but the sequence of things was all wrong and there was no food inside to make me feel less confused about this.

Hats for Dummies

A few conventionally attractive people were talking with each other at a party. None were making any sort of sexual advances toward another. None were in romantic relationships with one another. None were giving any sort of serious thought about what was happening after the party. They were talking about the ordinary looking people they knew. None were saying anything derogatory about ordinary looking people. None were disregarding an ordinary looking person's merit. None were implying that ordinary looking people maintained poor diets. The conventionally attractive people were just remarking that ordinary looking people were consumed with becoming more conventionally attractive. None were saying that it was an unworthy pursuit. None were referencing ordinary looking people's unsavory bone structure. None were giving any indication that they thought ordinary people should try to look more conventionally attractive by maybe buying a strategic hat. They were just making small talk. It was a party.

A few ordinary looking people were at the party, talking amongst themselves. They posed and directed their body language to indicate sexual efficiency. They laughed at funny jokes. They laughed at horrible jokes. They laughed really loudly. They drank too much punch. They excused themselves to the bathroom to squeeze zits. They tipped their hats but those aren't hats, they're hairpieces. They gave each other their cell phone numbers. They yelled out, "Hi how are you!" for no reason. Or maybe they had a reason. They tripped on their own dresses. They bruised their knees and it didn't matter. They laughed so hard it came out silent and their nostrils, well, their nostrils were moving really fast.

Narnia

There is a gigantic hole in the back of my fridge that leads to Narnia.

I would never go there. Narnia is for babies.

My Biggest Claim to Fame

My friend Jess was famous but she wasn't *that* famous. She wasn't as famous as Pamela Anderson, though her boobs were bigger and she was prettier and her hair was blonder.

"My hair is blonder," she said all the time, "Pamela stole the idea of platinum blonde from me, but I am blonder than she is." I think she was genuinely blonder.

Jess was famous enough to be recognized. People ran up to her and introduced themselves and then introduced her for her. She was that kind of famous. The kind where she didn't have to talk.

As friends, we mostly talked about her. We had an interesting conversation once about why she hated pickles. Her reasons were well-justified. She seemed maternal to me because she cursed a lot and always asked me if I was pregnant.

I showed up at her house one day and she was out in the pool wearing water wings as a bathing suit.

"I saw Pamela Anderson do that in a magazine before," I said.

"She stole the idea because she steals ideas from me." Her hair was blonde even when it was soaking wet. That's unnatural.

"Come and swim," she said, "you're irritating me by not swimming."

Cousins

1984–1987

Me and my four closest cousins –Erin, Becca, Jaime, and Joe – are born.

I live in Clearlake, and they each live within five miles of me.

1987

Our parents discover that Joe and I like to take our naps together on the floor.

They discover we both like bottles filled with juice.

They discover we both like bottles filled with unchilled jello water.

1988

Erin and I almost drown while trying to have an underwater tea party.

1989

Papa takes a long time in the bathroom; too long for us kids to wait. Nana gives us empty coffee cans and has us squat over them in the kitchen.

1990

I learn, during a game of hide-and-seek with my cousins, that my hearing can tell me what direction a voice is coming from when it yells 'ready!'

Erin and Becca go to Kindergarten. Aunt Ann encourages the rest of us to pretend we're sleeping right before they come home from school. They're disappointed when they find us sleeping because they want to play with us. I overuse the trick and it becomes useless.

Another close cousin, Adri, is born. The rest of us cousins take turns holding her while she cries. We hate waiting for our own turn, but holding her turns out to be not that exciting. We ignore her for a couple of years.

1991

Becca informs me and Joe about sex. She tells us to try it. We crawl under a bed and Joe lays on top of me. Becca doesn't know what's supposed to happen next. Joe has to go to the bathroom, so Becca lets him leave. We play ninja turtles when he gets back.

While walking our bikes up a hill to take into the carport, a car starts rolling down towards us. My trike stops it's tire, preventing it from running us over, but gets smashed in the process.

I refuse to take any more baths with Jaime because she always pees.

Nana Kopp dies, and I attend the funeral. None of my cousins go. I walk with my Nana, her daughter, up to her open casket. I am unaffected. A few weeks later, during a random case of watery eyes, my mom asks me what's wrong, and I lie and say I miss Nana Kopp. My mom cries.

During another random case of watery eyes, my mom asks me what's wrong, and I lie and say I miss Dylan, her boyfriend who moved away. She says she does too. Dylan soon moves back.

Becca and Erin teach me how to flare my nostrils.

We make a fort in the back yard. We design a boys' bathroom and a girls' bathroom. Our Nana finds out about that and tells us to stop being lazy and come inside when we have to pee. Someone poops in the girls' bathroom.

We decide that Becca and I are best friends, and Erin and Joe are best friends. We tell Jaime that she can be best friends with Adri.

1992

I discover, while watching Erin eat dinner, that when his mouth opens and closes, something near the ear moves, too. When I tell him, he says he already knows.

Erin tells me he found bugs in his Cheerios one time. I refuse to eat Cheerios for the next seven years.

Joe is terrified of a giant dinosaur blow-up toy that someone gave him for his birthday. The rest of us love it. We play with it, wrestle with it, climb on top of it, until it pops. Joe is terrified of its deflated carcass.

Jaime and I make up a cool laugh, and we both use it instead of our real laughs. One day, I say it sounds stupid and I stop doing it. She keeps using it. I'm upset that she didn't copy me and jealous that she still gets to use the laugh. I roll my eyes whenever she uses it. She never stops.

Our uncle teaches us how to pray. We think it's funny. We go to his bedroom and ask him to pray with us. When he isn't home, we read his sexist and racist joke books.

1993

Becca and I try to tell Adri about sex but she keeps saying 'six.'

Adri hates the skin of apples, so she lets me bite the skin off of her apples before she eats them. When she isn't looking, I take deep bites, but she usually notices. I think it's unfair that I don't get to eat the sweet part, but I don't ask for my own apples.

Becca and Joe move to Oregon.

I move to Washington. My mom says I can see Becca and Joe a lot again, but it doesn't really happen.

Becca and Joe's parents come to visit without Becca and Joe. I'm really irritated by this. I ask my aunt to play a game and she says she will. When she's in the bathroom I ask my uncle if she is really going to play and he tells me not to hold my breath. I'd never heard this expression.

1994

I move back to Clearlake.

Adri, Jaime and I have sleep-overs. Erin doesn't come because Joe isn't there to play with.

I remember the pretend-you're-sleeping joke and try it on Adri. I roll over in my fake sleep and she says she knows I'm not sleeping because I just moved. I fake wake up and drowsily ask what's going on. She says she knows I wasn't sleeping. I tell her, while rubbing my eyes, that people move around in their sleep all the time.

1995

I move to a neighboring town. Adri lives with my Nana and Papa, so I see her quite often when I visit them. I see Jaime occasionally, and Erin almost never.

I talk to Becca on the phone as often as I'm allowed.

My brother River is born on my birthday. Luckily we had my party the day before.

I develop an irrational fear for leaving the house without my mother. I have to be bribed to go to the fair with Adri and my aunt.

1996

Whenever Becca and Joe come down to visit, it takes me a while to remember how to talk to Becca. As soon as something funny happens, we laugh together and I remember how easy it is to talk to her and how much fun she is.

I see Erin for the first time in over a year. We're both at our Nana and Papa's house, and there are no other cousins. I want to talk to him, but I forget what we used to talk about. We entertain ourselves separately. Nana asks us to paint part of the porch railing. We talk and laugh together while we paint, and I remember how much I like him.

1997

Everyone goes to Nana and Papa's for Thanksgiving. Erin asks me and Becca if we want to smoke pot with him. We laugh and ignore him for the rest of the day. Our uncle is constantly mooning someone.

1998

Becca moves in with me. We share a room. I am jealous of the attention my mom gives her. I accuse her of using my razor blades to shave her legs. She moves back to Oregon.

1999

Becca moves in with our Nana and Papa. She goes to middle school with Jaime and Erin. She tells me Jaime likes to embarrass her in front of other kids.

2000

I move close to Erin and Jaime. I am the new girl at their small high school. Everyone calls me 'Erin's cousin.' I don't talk to him. I get the feeling he avoids me during breaks. His girlfriend is in my English class and I think she's cool. Someone tells me that before he dumped her, he got in one last fuck.

I move to a new town and change schools.

2001

Becca loses her virginity and tells her mom. Soon the whole family knows. I am too embarrassed to ask her about it.

2002

I move in with my Nana and Papa.

Becca moves in with my Nana and Papa and we share a room and go to high school together. It's exciting at first, but I begin to think she gets in the way of my social life. I avoid her during breaks.

Becca gets her GED and moves back to Oregon.

2004

I graduate high school and move to Oakland.

Becca and I both begin college. We halfheartedly try to convince each other to transfer to schools near our own. We talk on the phone less consistently.

2005

I see Jaime at a baby shower. I say 'Hi,' but nothing else. She doesn't introduce me to her boyfriend.

Joe stays with Nana and Papa for a while. I see him sometimes, and we get along really well. I ask him about his relationship history. I tell him I've always thought he was gay.

2006

Joe visits me in Oakland. He makes racist jokes and tells me he wants to fight the black guys who hang out around my apartment building.

I see Erin at Christmas and try to talk to him. He can't hold a conversation, stares blankly, eats with his fingers, and laughs to himself the whole time. I pretend I don't know he just got out of the mental hospital and ask him what he's been up to. He says 'not much.' He gives me a really good hug right before I leave.

Becca calls me crying one day. She says she's sorry for not calling me or answering my calls. She says she has a boyfriend and he is chronically depressed and has dropped out of school. She asks if I can come visit her. I can't.

I drop significantly on Becca's Myspace top friends.

2007

I visit Joe in Oregon and stay with him and his girlfriend at their apartment. They have a baby boy. Becca and her boyfriend come down with their baby and stay at Joe's apartment, too.

I see Jaime one day when I'm in town and we talk about childhood and I notice how different our vocabularies are.

I go to Oregon again, but no one answers the phone when I call.

Wait, Why are You in Denial?

There are two kinds of people in this world, I know I'm making a lot of generalizations. I think the only way to ever say anything real about the world is to make generalizations. But maybe that's a generalization. I should look up the word. Sometimes I meet someone who doesn't fit into any of my generalizations and I feel tongue-tied or something. I feel like I'm just standing there. Once I woke up with my mouth open and my cell phone in my hand ready to make a text message. It was scary. There are two types of people. There is the type of person who gets really afraid of the world when they think about their own anatomy, and there is the type of person who gets really afraid of the world when they think about outer space. I forget where I was going with that.

Insecurities in Cuties

It is Halloween and you and him are making candy apples. You say you can't eat any because you have some fake teeth, and that they might break on sticky candy. You show him the teeth by taking them out and laying them on the kitchen counter. He then shows you that each of his arm hairs is detachable.

If You Were Wondering if You're a Selfish Asshole

– Can I use that pen really quick?

– I'm using it.

– Sorry. I'll give it right back. I'm sorry.

– If you were wondering if you're a selfish asshole, then no, you're not. If anything, you're really nice. And not in a manipulative way. That's not what I'm saying.

– I'm not sure what you're saying. Here's the pen.

– I like that drawing. You're talented. And not in the pretentious way. I believe in you. I believe in Love and Positive Thinking and Global Warming and I believe in you.

– Thank you. I believe in you too.

– Have you ever fought a battle you knew you were going to lose?

– I fought a bakery once because they charged me fifty cents more for a loaf of bread than they usually did. I had been their customer for many years and was pretty disheartened by the price increase. But it turns out that the owner of the bakery had been giving me a discount all those years and had just forgotten to on that particular day.

– Do you still go to that bakery?

– No, but I want to.

– Have you fought any other battles?

– Why are you thinking about battles?

– I'm not really thinking very hard about battles. It's just that I was thinking about how bored I was and wishing that I were happier, or even *sadder*. I feel pretty convinced that I would feel better even if I was sadder. Boredom is the worst. Stagnation. That's another word for it.

– I see.

– But it sounds like a battle you can't win. Becoming sadder to improve overall mood. But I think that really is the case.

– I think you would feel differently if you were sad.

– No I wouldn't. I'm a little sad right now. Did you just flip that guy off?

– He was rubbing that girl's ass and staring at my chest.

– That seems rude.

– What were you saying?

– I think we should get lunch soon.

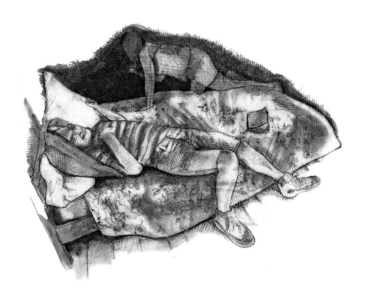

IF I WERE A POET THE FIRST THING I'D DO IS GET A REAL DARK TAN. JAVASCRIPT:VOID(0);

Puberty

Everyone was there, watching. Aunt Jackie. Katie and Marie. Mom. Grandma Billie and Grandma Mo. Todd. Aunt Rachel and Uncle Phil. The three neighbor kids who hadn't introduced themselves yet. The guy who had come to fix the roof. My friend Dennis. Aunt Rachel's best friend Amy on speakerphone.

I counted to ten. Then, when ten didn't work, I counted to twenty. I asked my mom how high she thought I should count. It's different for everyone, she said. Alright, I said. Then I counted to fifty.

Aunt Jackie and Aunt Rachel started talking about my posture and my quick temper. They were speaking in lowered voices, but everyone else was completely silent, so it was easy to hear them. Aunt Rachel mentioned that I had recently cried over the movie *She's All That*. It was disturbing, Aunt Rachel said. It's just the hormones, Aunt Jackie said. That, and all the counting.

My mom asked the guy who came to fix our roof if he had a cigarette. He said he didn't smoke and called my mom Lady. She told him to take his time with the roofing thing, it was no big deal, it was just a silly little thing, and that we were thinking of getting rid of the roof altogether. The man who came to fix the roof didn't answer and continued to stare at me.

I counted to one hundred.

I started to hear noises coming from someone's stomach, but no one said anything, then the noise stopped. A little while later I heard another stomach noise and someone said, Shh. One of the neighbor kids fell asleep on the couch.

Counting to two hundred was rough. I felt embarrassed. I began to develop a small fear that I would never stop counting. That this was my life now. This was who I was.

Uncle Phil asked me if I was a virgin. My mom told me I didn't have to answer that. I answered. Grandma Billie said she understood.

After I reached three hundred, Todd handed me a calculator. I cut my hair off really short like a boy and then regretted it. Pizza arrived mysteriously at the house and everyone ate. I fell asleep on the floor and when I woke up Aunt Jackie prompted me, You were at three hundred fifty.

OHMAGAH SERIOUSLAHH.

How to Save Money on Your Car Insurance

There is something really bad about sincerely believing that the world is getting ready to end. It almost feels like being on drugs. Like everything means exactly what it means and nothing means anything else and nothing is promised and you get what you get and one day you stop getting anything and you barely realize anything has changed. Sometimes I can convince myself that the world is not going to end, and then immediately convince myself that I will instead get a terrible disease and die anyways, alone, which is worse. I get panicky. I think, *Please let the world end before I get a terrible disease and die. That would be so humiliating.* Sometimes I want the world to end right now, not because I don't value life. I love living. It's just that, why continue when you know you can't make it to the end? When you can't tell your grandchildren all the stories you've been planning on telling them? I suppose you could just say your stories out loud, towards your ovaries, and think really hard about the potential ovaries of your little eggs and think of the eggs inside the potential ovaries as grandchildren. Then you might feel like you've told your grandchildren what you've been planning on telling them. But they won't remember, and I think memory is the most important part. It's like staying alive or something. It's like a sourdough starter. This is the story I want to tell my grandchildren:

Kids, I am your grandmother. Do you want to make me feel proud of you? There is one thing you need to know. You need, need, need to save money on your car insurance. That is key. I don't know what car insurance prices will be like when you're old enough to want car insurance, but maybe you will not even need a car. I heard they were going to start implanting microchips into people's brains that made brains more like computers. So maybe you won't even need a car because you won't need to drive to the café to check your email. Do you still use the term 'email'? Maybe it's archaic. Sometimes there are other reasons to need a car, such as if you're trying to find someone whose cell phone is turned off or if you need to go buy a new computer, but all of this should really be eliminated once everybody gets the microchips.

More Perfect and Less Idealistic

It was important that we rode the bus like this. Aimlessly. I was turning him into someone I would want to be friends with later when I needed friends. I was steering the conversation into something he could copy later, with me or with others. I was injecting my cynicism, my malleability, my disregard for social skills and physical appearance. I felt like there was no one in the whole world who cared about him as much as I did. I felt like I cared about no one else as much as I cared about him. He was mine momentarily and he was small and perfect, like a smaller more perfect version of myself, and we were in San Francisco and he was talking to me and I was trying really hard to pay attention. I wanted him to be mine and be small and look like me and seem fragile even with his glasses on and he was all of this, even without me.

Today is the Worst Day of My Entire Life (I Always Live in the Present)

I have seen actual eggs on the ground on hot days, not frying.

I have seen porta-potties turned over, no big deal.

I read once that a bruise larger than the size of one fourth of one's body is actually considered a broken bone.

I am considering reading Crime and Punishment for sport.

I am considering starting a Joy Luck Club.

I know Forrest Gump by heart.

I have been to Starbucks on purpose.

I have cut an umbilical cord.

I believe anything if it's written in Courier 12pt.

I know Home Alone by heart.

I believe that the easiest way to impress someone is by reciting lines from Home Alone spontaneously.

I think there is something really special about Play-doh that has never been handled.

I want to believe in Health Benefits.

I want to believe in Laughter Is The Best Medicine.

I want to ignore the dress code at work.

I want to start saving good text messages onto a zip drive.

I want to start proving complicated philosophical theories by flashing oncoming traffic and mocking celebrities.

I can't express my feelings fully.

I can't compete with Wal-Mart's prices.

I can't imagine myself in a world without Wal-Mart.

I like kids.

I am embarrassed about my naiveté.

I am embarrassed about certain pairs of my
underwear.
I am embarrassed about the dreadlock that's forming
in the back of my hair.
I am embarrassed about my mood sometimes when I'm
really moody.
I like the indoors a lot.
I like believing what people tell me.
I like believing that others believe I believe what they
tell me.
I think about what others think about me.
I think about people who I have no business thinking
about.
I think about my teacher from fourth grade, whose
voice was calming.
I feel afraid that I will die while spending time with
someone I don't like.
I feel afraid that I will die while in a state of boredom.
I don't ever want to die.
I don't ever want to choreograph a dance routine.
I don't ever want to be compared to Miley Cyrus.
I have lied several times in the last few minutes.
I have played Mortal Combat and won.
I have played Chinese checkers without knowing the
rules.
I have borrowed books and never returned them.
I copy answers when I don't feel like showing my work.
I design websites to keep track of my hormonal
fluctuations.
I design websites to attract potential mates.
I spend money irresponsibly to attract potential mates.
I trick potential mates into buying me alcohol.
I trick potential mates into writing love poems about me.
I might be getting a headache.
I might be watching an episode of Friends.
I might be paying someone else to write this for me.

I'd rather have nothing than something that isn't exactly what I want. —personal philosophy success story.

What the Tabloids are Saying About Me

"Martin looks ugly on Myspace. Doesn't she realize it?"

"Chealsea Martin gives a shit, we heard. She's into herself. She uses zit cream."

"Chelsea Martin is just like Ryan Seacrest only less beautiful, less popular, and less talented."

"Chelsea Martin is dating Ryan Seacrest, we heard. Or wait, Amy Winehouse is dating him."

"Amy Winehouse and Chelsea Martin are working on the next great American novel together and they both dumped Ryan Seacrest cos who the fuck is that, even?"

"Chelsea Martin just released her new book about herself. Big surprise."

"What is Chelsea Martin doing? Dressing weird? Where is her hat? Does she usually wear a hat?"

"Ack! Chelsea Martin did alcohol over the weekend! What was she thinking?!"

"Insider reports they heard Chelsea Martin talking to her current lover on her cell phone about an episode of that Kathy Griffin reality show. Wait, what Kathy Griffin reality show?"

"[Chelsea Martin] was spotted at Church's Chicken. Onlooker says she took over ten minutes to order one piece of breast meat to go.

The author would like to thank Kevin Sampsell, Megan Vrolijk, Brandon Gorrell, Jenn Lawrence, Julee Johnson, River Johnson, Kylie Martin-Johnson, Mike Young, William Schultz and Laurel Gunnarson.

Chelsea Martin was born in 1986 and grew up in Clearlake, California and currently lives in Oakland, California. She is a recent graduate of California College of the Arts.

To learn more about Chelsea Martin, visit her website at www.jerkethics.com

Other Books from Future Tense

Embrace Your Insignificance:
Lessons Learned Teaching English in Japan *by Bob Gaulke, $11*

Our Beloved 26th *by Riley Michael Parker, $3*

Double Header: A Flip Book *by Suzanne Burns, $5*

Partial List of People to Bleach *by Gary Lutz, $6*

The Haiku Inferno Book *by Haiku Inferno, $8*

Before You She Was a Pitbull *by Elizabeth Ellen, $5*

Dahlia Season: A Novella & Stories *by Myriam Gurba, $14.95*

Don't Take Your Life *by Justin Maurer, $5*

Fast Forward: Confessions of a Porn Screenwriter
by Eric Spitznagel, $13.95

The Heart Is Also a Furnace *by Magdalen Powers, $5*

Future Tense Books
PO Box 42416
Portland, OR 97242

For quicker service, order from our website
www.futuretensebooks.com

CPSIA information can be obtained
at www.ICGtesting.com
Printed in the USA
FSOW01n1529140815
9736FS